The Grumpy Bunny® All Year Long

by Justine Korman ● illustrated by Lucinda McQueen

The Grumpy Bunny Goes to School

The Grumpy Bunny's Spooky Night

Grumpy Bunny's Snowy Day

I Love You, Grumpy Bunny

The Grumpy Bunny's Too Many Bunnybabies

The Grumpy Easter Bunny

SCHOLASTIC INC.

New York Toronto London Auckland Sydney
Mexico City New Delhi Hong Kong Buenos Aires

The Grumpy Bunny®
Goes to School

For Patsy Jensen, an editor who's never grumpy
— J.K.

For Abby Guitar—Lots of love from Aunt Lucy

Hopper woke up to a perfect September day. Orange and gold leaves twirled in the fresh fall breeze. The sky was a bright, clear blue.

But Hopper felt grumpy. In fact, the grumpy bunny was even grumpier than usual because today was the first day of school.

Once again, Hopper would be helping Mrs. Clover teach the kinderbunny class at Easter Bunny Elementary School. That was where young bunnies went to learn how to be Easter Bunnies.

The new bunnies were always very excited. But to Hopper, school was just the same old ho-hum, humdrum thing.

First the bunnies would gather around
the Great Tree while the chief of all the Easter
Bunnies, Sir Byron the Great Hare, would lead
them in the Easter Bunny's Pledge:

Making treats with care and art,
Bringing love to every heart,
Spreading sunshine every day,
That's the Easter Bunny way!

Then all the eager, scared, happy young bunnies would hop off to their classes. Mrs. Clover always started the day with egg coloring. She taught the same patterns every year: straight lines and flowers, all just so. Then came marshmallow puffing and basket weaving.

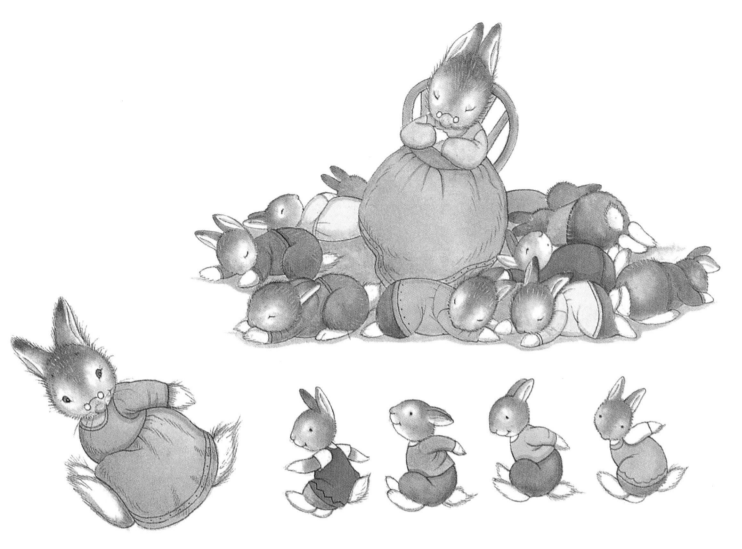

The three-carrot snack would be followed by a nap,
then hippety-hop drills, wheelbarrow practice, and, finally,
treat hiding.

Hopper sighed. It was time to go. In fact, the first schoolbunnies were already gathering around the Great Tree as Hopper dragged himself down the path to school. His poor feet felt very tired.

How will I ever get through all those boring hippety-hop drills? he wondered miserably.

Hopper reached the Great Tree just as the schoolbunnies were finishing the pledge. He put his paw over his heart and muttered, "Spreading sunshine, and all that ho-hum, humdrum."

Suddenly Hopper realized Sir Byron was looking right at him!

"I'm sorry I was late," Hopper began.

But Sir Byron said, "No time for that now. You've got a class to teach. Mrs. Clover is sick. You're on your own today."

Hopper's ears flew up in surprise. "What? That's not fair!" he started to complain. Then Hopper had an idea.

"Well, perhaps I could get someone else . . ." Sir Byron began.

But Hopper shook his head. "Never mind, sir. I'll be fine." And he hopped off before the Great Hare could wonder why the grumpy bunny wasn't being grumpy anymore.

Hopper hopped toward the kinderbunny room. *Today I can do things my way!* he thought happily.

And that's just what Hopper did! First he painted the craziest-looking egg anyone had ever seen.

Then Hopper told the kinderbunnies, "Paint your eggs however you want. Just make them as pretty as you can."

The kinderbunnies went far beyond stripes and flowers.
They painted designs Hopper had never even imagined. There
were star-spangled eggs, rainbow eggs, and eggs
with leopard spots. One even grinned like a
bright orange jack-o'-lantern.

Hopper didn't hand out patterns for the baskets. Instead, he just gave the kinderbunnies pieces of straw and said, "Weave the baskets however you want. The colors and shapes are up to you. Just make them as beautiful as you can."

When it came time for the marshmallow puffing, Hopper didn't make the usual speech about being careful not to puff too much. He decided to let the kinderbunnies find out for themselves.

PUFF, PUFF, they puffed up their chicks . . .

. . . till one bunny named Peter puffed too much.

PA-WUFFFF! Marshmallow went flying everywhere!

"Let's all do that!" the other bunnies shrieked happily.

"All right," Hopper said. "But see if you can tell exactly when the chick is about to explode. That way you'll learn how much puffing is too much."

A few minutes later, Hopper asked the sticky bunnies to gather together. "You all know how to hippety-hop," he began. "Now try to hoppety-hip. Because once you can hoppety-hip, hippety-hopping is a snap."

"It's hard," a kinderbunny named Daisy said.
"No, it's fun!" cried her friend Flopsy.

When the bunnies were tired of hoppety-hipping, Hopper said, "Every Easter Bunny must learn to push a wheelbarrow filled with treats. We could march our wheelbarrows back and forth across the room—or we could have a race!"

The kinderbunnies cheered. Soon they were racing around the room, laughing with glee.

Just then Sir Byron appeared. "What's all this noise?" shouted the Great Hare.

Every bunny fell silent. Hopper's ears dropped and his stomach flippety-flopped. "Um, I . . ." the nervous bunny stammered.

"We were having a wheelbarrow race!" shouted Flopsy.

One look at Sir Byron's angry face and Hopper knew he was in deep trouble. He looked down at his sore feet and wished he'd never gotten out of bed.

Sir Byron looked around the marshmallow-strewn room. "What's all this mess?" he asked.

Hopper didn't know what to say. "I . . . we . . ."

"We made our chicks so puffy they exploded!" Peter cried. "*PA-WUFFFF!*" he added, puffing up his furry cheeks.

Hopper groaned. This day was getting worse by the minute.

Then Sir Byron spotted the eggs drying on the windowsill. "And what happened here? Did you forget to show them the proper painting patterns?"

Daisy said, "Hopper let us paint whatever we wanted. It was fun!"

"I see," said the Great Hare. Then he stared at the eggs. "Some of these are actually quite pretty."

Hopper's ears lifted. Had he heard Sir Byron right?

"Tradition is good. But there's always room for new ideas," the Great Hare declared. "A wheelbarrow race might help improve their skills—and the bunnies certainly seemed to enjoy it. And perhaps letting the bunnies explode a few marshmallows is the best way to teach them when to stop puffing," the Great Hare added.

Hopper's jaw dropped. Sir Byron clapped him on the back. "You'll make a fine teacher someday, Hopper. In the future, though, I hope you'll bring your ideas to me first."

Hopper nodded eagerly. He still couldn't quite believe that he wasn't in trouble.

"Of course, you'll have to clean up this mess," the Great Hare said.

Hopper's heart sank. It would take him all afternoon to clean up the sticky room.

Then Daisy said, "We'll help you, Hopper."
"Yes!" Flopsy cried. "You're our favorite teacher!"
"Even cleaning up will be fun with you!" Peter declared.
And, to Hopper's amazement, it was.

Hopper hippety-hopped all the way home. He was so happy that even his sore feet felt good!

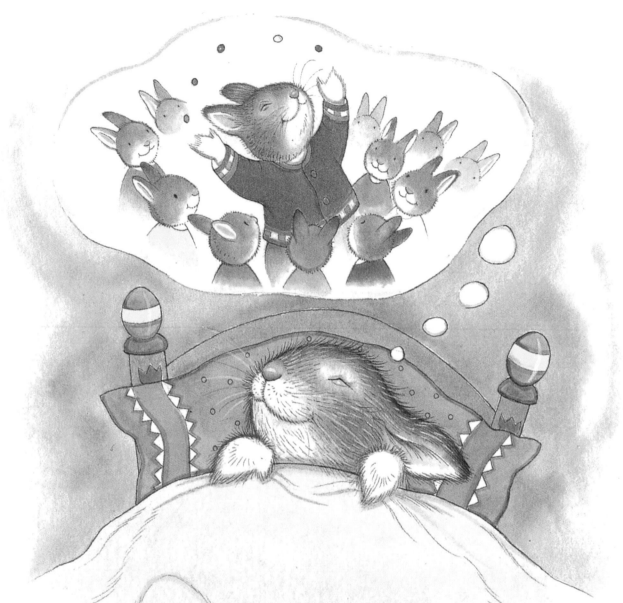

Back in his burrow, Hopper decided, "Tomorrow I'll ask Sir Byron if I can teach jellybean juggling."

He couldn't wait to go back to school the next day. In fact, from that day on, Hopper was never grumpy about going to school again.

The
Grumpy Bunny's®
Spooky Night

For Ron, who taught me the art of Halloween.
It's scary how much I love you!
—J.K.

For my favorite goblins, Katy and Eric,
who've loved their spooky Salem nights!
Lots of love, Lucy

Hopper grumbled as he led the kinderbunnies to the Easter Bunny Elementary School auditorium. "Dumbest holiday of the year," said the grumpy bunny. "The only thing scary about Halloween is how much time and effort critters waste on it."

"Our school is proud to welcome a new art and drama teacher," Sir Byron announced. "For his first production, Mr. Spumoni will be creating a haunted house in my barn. Lilac has volunteered to provide the music. But we need one class to help with the work. That lucky class will enjoy a special Halloween sleepover in the barn!"

As eager kinderbunnies tugged at Hopper's coat, the grumpy bunny saw the dashing drama teacher smile at Lilac. Both of Hopper's paws flew up in the air. He wanted to be wherever Lilac was!

The next thing Hopper knew, he and the kinderbunnies were at Sir Byron's barn. "What a dump!" Hopper muttered.

"Perhaps it is now." Mr. Spumoni spread his cape grandly. "But through the magic of paint and imagination—a true House of Horrors!"

"First we sweep!" Mr. Spumoni commanded.

While Hopper was sweeping, a big spider suddenly swung down into his face. "AI-YEE!" the grumpy bunny screamed.

Mr. Spumoni rushed over.

Hopper blushed. "I'm fine. The spider just surprised me."

Mr. Spumoni clapped him on the back. "That's brilliant! We'll create Spider City—a giant spider swings down and attacks! You build it!"

"But I don't know how to build a spider city!" Hopper groaned.
"Some boxes. Pipe cleaners. You'll figure it out," Mr. Spumoni said.

To the grumpy bunny's surprise, he did!

Hopper built a giant spider out of four pairs of tights, some packing peanuts, and glow-in-the-dark paint.

He even got the spider to swing down on cue!

"This theater stuff is kind of fun," Hopper admitted to Lilac. "But these corny tricks won't scare anyone."

Hopper helped the kinderbunnies make paper-towel ghosts and black paper bats. "How could someone be scared of some paper towels and—"

"—the magic of lights, music, theater!" Mr. Spumoni concluded for him. "You'll see tonight!"

Mr. Spumoni told the kinderbunnies to come back after dark dressed in their costumes.

"What are you going to wear?" Lilac asked Hopper.

"I never wear costumes," the grumpy bunny declared.

"You will tonight," Mr. Spumoni said. "Teachers must set an example."

"No, I . . ." Hopper started to object.

But with a swirl of his cape, the drama teacher was gone!

"I can't wear costumes," Hopper told Lilac. "Whenever I do, something goes wrong, and everybunny laughs at me."

That night Hopper "forgot" to wear a costume. But Mr. Spumoni brought an extra. "Just for you, Mr. Hopper," he said.

Hopper wasn't pleased, but he couldn't disappoint Lilac.

"You will be the host, Mr. Clown," Mr. Spumoni explained. "You'll lead groups through the haunted house. If anyone gets too scared, you'll make them laugh."

Hopper scoffed. Who would be scared of a bit of paint and nonsense?

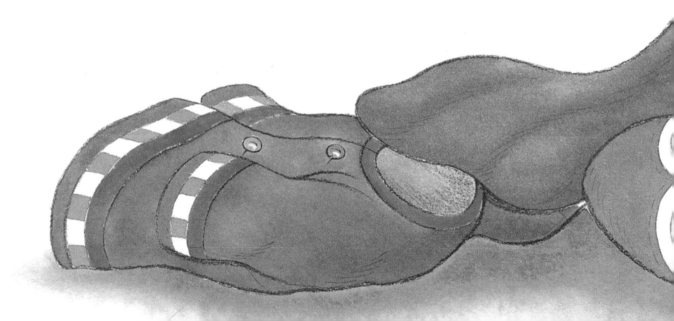

But when he walked in with the first group of visitors, Hopper couldn't believe his eyes. In the dark, with Lilac's eerie music playing and all the kinderbunnies in costumes and makeup, he hardly recognized the old barn!

"Get them off me!" somebunny cried as the paper bats swooshed down over the cardboard graveyard.

Hopper juggled jellybeans
until the audience had calmed
down enough to visit the
Creepy Café.

When the ghoulish waiter lifted the lid to reveal Bingo's head on a plate, the crowd leaped back in horror!

And when the tour reached Spider City . . .

"AI-YEE!" Hopper screamed. In all the excitement, he'd forgotten his own trick!

"Wonderful scream!" Mr. Spumoni whispered. "You're a showman at heart!" After that, Hopper screamed for each tour, just to keep the crowd jumping.

At the end of the night, Sir Byron announced, "This haunted house has been a huge success, thanks to all of you!"

The kinderbunnies cheered. Even Hopper had to admit, "Halloween can be fun, even if it isn't scary."

"The show is over! Let's strike the set and get some sleep!" Mr. Spumoni declared.

By the time everything was put away and the kinderbunnies had spread out their sleeping bags, Hopper was exhausted. But the kinderbunnies were still full of excitement and candy.

"I want another drink of water!" Peter said.

"Flopsy stole my candy bar!" Mopsy cried.

"It was mine!" Flopsy insisted.

Hopper settled arguments, fluffed pillows, and delivered many glasses of water before—FINALLY!—the kinderbunnies got sleepy. As they snuggled into their sleeping bags, Mr. Spumoni told them some spooky Halloween stories.

Then, just as the grumpy bunny prepared to settle down for the night, Lilac had a request. "Oh, Hopper, I left my toothbrush in the car. Can you get it for me, please?"

Hopper was so tired he could barely stand on his sore feet. But, of course, he would do anything for Lilac.

Hopper found the toothbrush and came back to the barn. Alone in the dark, he felt just a teeny bit scared. *That's silly,* he told himself. *There's no such thing as . . .*

GHOSTS! The barn was full of ghosts!

For just one second, Hopper believed! A chill shivered up his spine. Then he realized it was just the kinderbunnies' paper-towel ghosts, artfully lit by Mr. Spumoni's flashlight.

The grumpy bunny laughed sheepishly.

"Were you scared, my friend?" Mr. Spumoni asked.

Hopper's spine still felt all tingly and tickly. The fur on his ears stood on end.

"That's not as scary as what we'll do next year!" Mr. Spumoni continued. "I picture a sunken pirate ship . . . blue lights, sea songs . . ."

"And a giant octopus!" Hopper couldn't wait to build it!

As he drifted off to dreamland, Hopper wondered, what does Halloween mean?

A special night to play pretend
and dress up, if you dare.
Lights! Magic! Candy! Thrills!
And, just for fun, a scare!

Grumpy Bunny's SNOWY DAY

For Monkey Boy,
who makes every day fun!
—J.K.

For Kaylee and Jamie,
who always enjoy their snowy days
Love, Lucy

One morning, Hopper woke up to a winter wonderland. But was the grumpy bunny happy? Of course not!

"Boots and bother," Hopper grumbled. He hated all the fuss of snow. And most of all, Hopper hated shoveling!

While he ate breakfast, Hopper listened to the radio:
"Due to last night's storm, the following schools will be closed: Bitty Bunny Preschool, Easter Bunny Elementary School . . ."

The grumpy bunny sighed with relief. At least he wouldn't have to go to school and be pestered by a bunch of excited kinderbunnies.

Hopper pulled on his coat, boots, hat, scarf, and mittens. "What a lot of stuff to wear," he complained. "Once I get all this shoveling done, I'll come inside and have a nice, quiet day at home."

But as soon as the grumpy bunny stepped outside, he was surrounded by snow-happy kinderbunnies.

Little Muffin laughed. "Isn't it beautiful?"

"Happy snow day, Hopper," Peter called.

Hopper grunted. He saw nothing happy about having to shovel.

Suddenly, his ears flew up with an idea. What if he got the kinderbunnies to shovel for him? After all, those silly little bunnies found fun in everything. They would probably even enjoy shoveling.

Hopper turned to his students.

"Hot chocolate all around—if you shovel my walk," he proposed.

The kinderbunnies looked skeptical. "We can get hot chocolate at home without shoveling," Muffin pointed out.

Peter thought for a moment, then he smiled at Hopper. "We'll shovel your walk, *if* you take us sledding down the Big Hill first."

"I don't know," muttered Hopper. "That doesn't sound like such a good idea to me."

"Please!" said all the kinderbunnies together. "Pretty please with marshmallows on top!"

"Oh, all right," Hopper grumped. "Let's get this over with." He and the kinderbunnies tramped through the sparkling snow to the Big Hill.

"Okay, hurry up and have fun!"
Hopper announced when they reached the top of the Big Hill.
"We won't be here long!"

But no one was listening. The kinderbunnies were already
sledding down the long, steep hill, squealing with glee.

Hopper watched their first few runs. None of the bunnies was going as far or as fast as he knew he could.

He reached for Peter's sled. "Here, let me show you the right way to do it," he said.

Hopper ran as fast as he could, then flopped onto the sled. Soon he was whooshing full-speed down the Big Hill.

By the time Hopper saw the snowdrift, it was too late. He wiped out in a cascade of powdery snow. It was wonderful!

Hopper couldn't wait to go again.
As he pulled the sled back up the hill,
his ears bounced merrily with
each step.

Finally, everyone was all tuckered out. "Let's go shovel the walk now," said Hopper, and all the kinderbunnies agreed. But on the shortcut back to Hopper's house, the group passed a frozen pond.

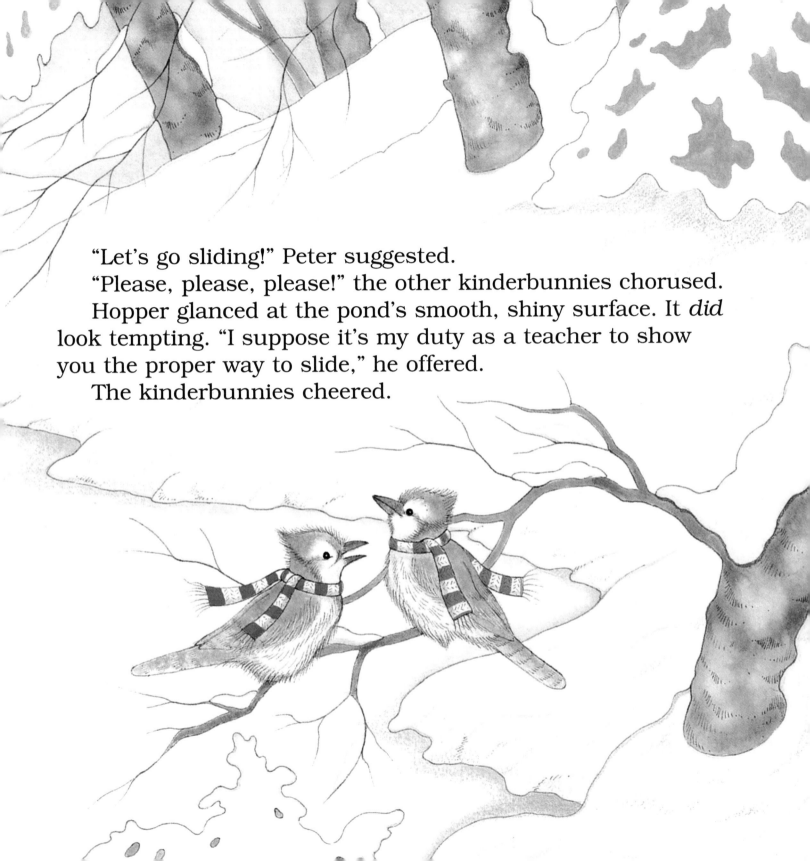

"Let's go sliding!" Peter suggested.

"Please, please, please!" the other kinderbunnies chorused.

Hopper glanced at the pond's smooth, shiny surface. It *did* look tempting. "I suppose it's my duty as a teacher to show you the proper way to slide," he offered.

The kinderbunnies cheered.

Hopper got a running start. When he had picked up
enough speed, he jumped onto the ice and slid. The world
rushed past him in a blur of shimmering snow. For a moment,
he felt as if he were flying!

Then his foot hit a rock poking up through the ice. Hopper stuck out his arms, wiggled his ears, and recovered his balance. "I've still got it!" he cried triumphantly as he—

FA-WHUMP! Hopper felt hard, cold ice under his tail.
As he skidded to a stop, he heard a funny sound:
FA-FA-FA . . .WHUMP, WHUMP, WHUMP!
The kinderbunnies who had been sliding behind Hopper tumbled into one another like falling dominoes.
Flopsy laughed, and everyone joined in—even Hopper!

The group left the pond and began to walk back to
Hopper's house. But all that deep white snow was just
too enticing.

"Let's have a snowball fight!" Muffin shouted.

The other bunnies ran to a big drift to build their forts.

Hopper forgot all about shoveling. He loved snowball fights!

The grumpy bunny cleared his throat. "I suppose I *should*
teach you the right way to build a snow fort."

He showed the kinderbunnies how to shape mounds of
snow into sturdy shelters.

After Hopper and the kinderbunnies had built their forts, he taught them how to pack a perfect snowball.

Soon the bunnies were caught up in a fierce battle. Snowballs whizzed through the air. Bunnies from one fort tried to sneak up on the other. Walls were battered and rebuilt. Targets were bombarded. Mittens were soaked.

Two kinderbunnies grabbed big round
snowballs and came running at Hopper.
"Watch this dodge," he said, diving to one side.
Suddenly, he found himself staring up at the sky.
Hopper had fallen backward onto the soft snow.

He waved his arms up and down and scissored
his legs in and out.

"Snow angels!" the kinderbunnies exclaimed. They all
fell down in the snow and joined in.

Hopper and the kinderbunnies made snow angels all
the way back to Hopper's house.

"Now it really is time for shoveling," Hopper declared.
With all the kinderbunnies pitching in, shoveling wasn't
boring at all. In fact, Hopper had to admit—it was fun!

First, they had a speed-shoveling race. Then there was a contest to see who could throw snow the highest and who could pitch it the farthest.

Once all the snow was in a giant heap,
Hopper looked at it and had a wonderful
thought. "Let's build a snowbunny!"
The kinderbunnies were happy
to help.

In no time at all, the spectacular statue was done. But something was missing. "I think he needs some friends," Hopper suggested.

The bunnies worked quickly, and soon the big snowbunny was surrounded by lots of little snowbunnies. Hopper grinned. "That's much better."

"I sure hope it snows tomorrow!" Daisy said.

"Me, too!" Flopsy cried.

"Me, three!" the other bunnies cheered.

And to his amazement, Hopper agreed. "I have an idea," he said. "Let's do a snowdance."

Peter was confused. "A snowdance?"

"You know—like a raindance, only for snow," Flopsy explained.

But Hopper had already begun. He weaved between the snow-covered trees, throwing his head back to look at the sky.
They danced till they were dizzy and all the parents throughout the woods started calling the kinderbunnies to come home.

"Thanks for a wonderful day!" the kinderbunnies said as they hopped away.

"Thank *you!*" said Hopper.

And as he watched them leave, Hopper remembered a rhyme he'd learned back when *he* was a kinderbunny at Easter Bunny Elementary School:

> *No matter what the weather brings,*
> *an Easter Bunny makes it spring.*
> *Find sunshine in every day—*
> *That's the Easter Bunny way!*

I Love You, Grumpy Bunny®

For my grumpy valentine with love
—J.K.

For Jeremy—Your always valentine, Lucy

It was the day before Valentine's Day, and Hopper the bunny was even grumpier than usual. All his kinderbunny students at Easter Bunny Elementary School were shrieking with glee as they made messy valentines for their friends and families.

"Who needs candy and flowers and all that sappy stuff?" Hopper grumbled to himself. "I can't wait until Valentine's Day is over. It's the corniest holiday of the year!"

When Hopper was leaving the school that day, Coach Cornelius bounded up to him. Coach was one of the school's two gym teachers.

"Hey, Hopper!" he called in a booming voice. "Will you help me make a valentine for Marigold? You're smart about stuff like that."

Marigold was the other gym teacher at the school.

Hopper hated the whole idea of valentines. But he didn't know how to say no to Coach.

"Oh, all right," the grumpy bunny sighed. "What do you want to—"

Just then Hopper heard a voice as sweet as a spring breeze. Lilac, the music teacher, was singing as she hopped down the school steps. She was always singing, humming, or laughing. Hopper thought Lilac was the most wonderful bunny in the world.

"Good-bye, Coach," said Lilac. "Have a great afternoon, Hopper," she added sweetly.

Hopper wanted to say something, but all he could do was blush until Lilac was gone.

"So what should I say in my valentine?" Coach asked
Hopper.

"Well, let's start with the basics," said Hopper. "What do
you like about Marigold?"

Coach thought for a second. "She's lots of fun!" he said.

Hopper sighed. "Can you be more specific?" he asked. "I mean, if I was writing a valentine to, say, Lilac, I would talk about the way she gets everyone to sing, even the shyest kinderbunnies, or the way she tilts her ears when she's listening, or the way her laugh sounds like music..." Hopper's voice trailed off dreamily.

Coach chuckled. "Maybe you should write a valentine, too."
"Who, me? Never!" Hopper scoffed. "Besides, there's no way
someone like Lilac would ever want to be my valentine."

"You'll never find out if you don't ask her," Coach said.
"You know what I always say: Try, try, try—win!"
"Don't coach me, Coach," Hopper grumbled. "Besides,
I thought *I* was supposed to be helping *you*."

Coach shrugged. "OK," he said. "So how do I tell Marigold she's fun?"

"Flowers? Candy?" Hopper suggested.

Coach bounced his basketball and said, "Marigold doesn't like that stuff any more than I do."

Hopper snapped his fingers. "I've got it! Let's write a valentine on a basketball!"

Coach grinned. "You are smart! But what can I say?"

Hopper thought for a minute. "How about this?

You're my favorite gal of all.
You're more fun than basketball!"

Coach was so happy, he punched Hopper on the arm, then gave him a high five.

"That's perfect! Thanks, Hopper! You're a real poet," Coach said. With that, he jumped out of the house, leaving Hopper a little confused and a bit squished.

A poet—me? Well, maybe I could give it a try, Hopper thought. So he wrote a valentine to Lilac.

Hopper was surprised to find that making a valentine was actually fun! He even trimmed it with lace and added glitter and a bow.

Now Hopper couldn't wait for Valentine's Day, when he could give Lilac his wonderful card.

The next morning, Hopper happily skipped to school. He ran inside early—and bumped right into Lilac!

Hopper wanted to give her the valentine. He wanted to say, "Will you be mine?" But instead he just stood there, frozen with fear and quiet as a carrot.

"Happy Valentine's Day, Hopper!" Lilac sang as she hopped into her classroom.

I was just surprised to see her, Hopper thought. *I'll give Lilac the valentine at lunch.*

But by lunchtime, Hopper had grown even more nervous. In fact, he was so nervous, he tripped and dropped his tray with a loud *CRASH!*

Several schoolbunnies burst out laughing. But Lilac didn't laugh. She gave Hopper half her sandwich.

Hopper was too nervous to eat—and much too nervous to give Lilac the valentine.

"I'm too nervous even to talk!" Hopper said to himself.

But then Hopper had a great idea.
I don't have to ask Lilac to be my valentine, he thought.
I'll just sneak the card into her classroom and leave it for her!
He jumped up and hurried out of the lunch room.

Luckily, the music room was empty. Hopper put the valentine on Lilac's music stand. She was sure to see it there.

Suddenly, Hopper had a thought, and he felt nervous all over again. What if someone else saw the valentine, too? Or what if Lilac thought it was dumb? Or what if...

Hopper grabbed the valentine and crumpled it up. Then he tossed it in the trash.

"Who am I kidding?" he grumbled to himself. "No one would want to be my valentine!"

Hopper was so busy grumbling, he didn't even notice Lilac coming down the hall.

Hopper was especially grumpy the rest of the day.
After school came the worst part of all—the Valentine's Day party. Hopper looked around at all the pretty decorations and happy schoolbunnies exchanging cards and sharing pink cupcakes. His bottom lip trembled a little as he mumbled, "Valentine's Day stinks!"

Then Lilac stepped up on the stage and sat down at the piano. "I have a special treat for you today," she announced. "This is an original Valentine's Day song written by a very talented bunny."

Lilac began to play. "Your voice is sweet like candy treats," she sang.

Hopper's ears perked up at the very first line. It was his valentine to Lilac! She had set his poem to music.

Hopper felt himself blushing from head to toe. He also felt as if he would burst with pride—especially at the end of the song, when the schoolbunnies clapped and Lilac winked at him.

After the applause, Hopper walked up to Lilac shyly. "I guess you found my card," he said with an embarrassed grin. "Yes," said Lilac sweetly. "It was beautiful."

"I wanted to, um, ask you something," said Hopper. "Would you, um, be my, um, valentine?"
Lilac grinned. "I thought you'd never ask!"

As Hopper and Lilac left the school together, they saw
Coach and Marigold playing basketball.

"Hi, guys!" called Coach. While his back was turned,
Marigold sneaked by him toward the basket.

"Yes!" shouted Marigold, watching the ball swish through
the hoop. "Two points!"

All the bunnies laughed.

Hopper smiled at Lilac, who smiled back at him. The grumpy bunny had never felt so un-grumpy.

"Valentine's Day turned out to be pretty wonderful after all," Hopper said to himself that night. In fact, Hopper was so happy that he made up a new verse for the Easter Bunny pledge:

Who cares if valentines are sappy,
As long as they make someone happy?
And every bunny ought to know
A valentine will help love grow!

The Grumpy Bunny's®
Too Many Bunnybabies

For my parents, Marvin & Eleanore, who read to me.
In the fond hope that they'll someday read to their grandchildren.
—J.K.

For Roy, always a true gentleman and a wonderful person to work with!
Warm regards and many thanks.
—L.M.

As soon as school was done for the day, Hopper the grumpy bunny hurried to see his favorite friend, Lilac. But the pretty music teacher was on her way out. "I'm going to read at the Bunnybaby Center's storytime," Lilac explained.

"How can you read to babies?" Hopper grumbled. "They don't understand you!"

"Bunnybabies love stories!" Lilac said. "And reading to them now makes babies good readers when they grow up."

"Why don't you come in and see?" Lilac suggested.
So Hopper followed her into the Easter Bunny Elementary School's Bunnybaby Center.

Lilac introduced Hopper to Mrs. Milkweed, who took care of
the bunnybabies.

Mrs. Milkweed soon had all the little ones settled in a circle
on the floor, and Lilac began to read them a story.

But before she could finish the first book, the music teacher got a phone call.

"My sister is having her babies! I've got to go to the hospital!" she exclaimed.

Lilac turned to Hopper. "Can you take over?"

Hopper wasn't so sure about finishing Lilac's storytime. But Mrs. Milkweed had her paws full, and no one else was around to help.

Reluctantly Hopper started reading.
But the bunnybabies had other ideas. . . .

Dandylion threw a book!

Flora took off her diaper and waved it like a flag!

Alfalfa ate a page!

"Oh, nettles and burrs!" Mrs. Milkweed exclaimed.
"The wee ones always get a bit fussy before their nap."
A bit fussy?! Hopper thought. This was chaos!
The bunnybabies had gotten into the books and
toys—and they were out of control!

"They're great little readers once they get settled,"
Mrs. Milkweed assured Hopper. "Could you help, please?"

As Hopper looked around at the bunnybabies, his first thought was to hop away as fast as his feet would take him. But then he remembered Lilac and knew she was counting on him.

So while Mrs. Milkweed fed Alfalfa, Hopper
tried to keep Dandylion off the bookshelf
and get Flora into a clean diaper.

Unfortunately, Flora wasn't the only bunnybaby who needed a new diaper. "Grrr-oss!" Hopper grumbled.

Finally, all the bunnybabies were settled back in their circle.

Once again, Hopper began to read—and this time the bunnybabies listened.

They giggled when Hopper used funny voices.

They looked at the pictures.

They even seemed to understand!

After three stories, Mrs. Milkweed handed Hopper a bedtime book. "They love to hear this one before their nap," she explained.

Hopper read the gentle bedtime tale and . . .

. . . dozed off himself! Soon he was having an amazing dream. He saw books and bunnybabies . . . bunnybabies and books. . . .

Suddenly Lilac appeared in Hopper's dream. "Hopper," she said, "I'm an aunt! I'm an aunt six times over!"

"You can't be an ant. You're a bunny," Hopper grumbled.

When he heard Lilac giggle, the grumpy bunny woke up.
Lilac looked admiringly at the happy, comfortable
bunnybabies. "And since you're so good with little ones,
I'm sure you'll want to help with the baby-sitting,"
she said.

Me? Good with bunnybabies? Hopper thought.
Then he grinned. Maybe he was! And despite the diapers,
Hopper had to admit that the little ones were lots of fun!

"Sure, I'll babysit," he agreed.

That's when Hopper had a truly scary thought. Maybe someday he would even have bunnybabies of his own!

All bunnybabies need these things:
Clean diapers, milk, and toys.
But books are also something great
for little girls and boys!

The Grumpy®
Easter Bunny

For Ron, the grumpiest bunny of all
—J.K.

For Alex Guitar
—Lots of love from Aunt Lucy

Deep in the forest on
the night before Easter, the bunnies
danced under the moon. They were all as
happy as …well, Easter bunnies—except for one
grumpy bunny named Hopper.

After the bunnies had finished dancing, Sir Byron, the Great Hare, told them, "You are the messengers of spring. Go now, and spread love and joy!"

Hopper kicked a stone and grumbled, "Joy and love. Ha! I hate that mushy stuff."

As he waited in line for his wheelbarrow full of
Easter treats, Hopper grew even grumpier. What was the
point of making treats all year and then running your
paws off to hide them for someone else to find?

While the other bunnies gladly began their rounds, Hopper dragged his already tired feet.

Hopper gazed at the heap of chocolate bunnies, marshmallow chicks, caramels, raspberry creams, and other delights.

"I wish all these treats were mine," he thought hungrily.

Then his ears flew up with a wicked idea.
"They *could* be mine!" he said. "Who will
ever know if I keep the goodies or give
them away?"

Hopper ran to his burrow, pushing the
heavy wheelbarrow as fast as he could.

Hopper tried to roll the heavy wheelbarrow inside, but it was too wide. He pushed and shoved and pushed some more.

He was so busy pushing, Hopper didn't notice a strawberry-cream-filled egg fall off the wheelbarrow. The egg rolled down the shady path toward the stream.

Hopper puffed up his tiny chest. Then he pushed with all his might. The wheelbarrow lurched forward, and the grumpy bunny fell flat on his face.

"That was almost as hard as delivering the treats," Hopper complained.

But at last, the goodies were inside. Hopper ran his paws through the mountain of candy. He juggled jellybeans and made marshmallow nests for the chocolate eggs.

Then he began to eat.

And eat.

And eat!

Hopper gobbled and gnawed the whole night through. Now he didn't feel so grumpy, but he did feel very sticky and a little too full.

Finally, he decided to go to the stream to get a nice, cool drink.

Hopper stopped when he heard a *mew, mew, mew.* He peeked out from behind a tree and saw Lottie, Spottie, and Dottie, three kittens who lived nearby.

Hopper hid in the
reeds and listened.
"They must be here
somewhere," Spottie mewed.
"This *is* Easter morning,
isn't it?" Lottie asked.
"Oh, dear," Hopper thought. "The kittens are
searching for Easter treats—and they aren't going to
find any!"

Hopper felt an uncomfortable stirring deep
inside. Should he have eaten the treats? Had he
done the wrong thing?

Then, to Hopper's great surprise, Dottie cried, "I found one!"

She had found the strawberry-cream-filled egg that had fallen off his wheelbarrow.

Before Hopper could say a word, Spottie and Lottie rushed to their sister.

"I'm the oldest," Spottie said, grabbing for the egg.

"I'm the hungriest," Lottie argued.

"I found it!" Dottie squeaked.

Hopper felt terrible as
he watched the kittens wrestle
and hiss in the dewy grass.
   Suddenly, the kittens rolled right
over the egg and smashed it to bits. They
stopped wrestling and stared at the gooey mess.

"We should have shared," Spottie mewed sadly.
"We shouldn't have been greedy," Lottie sighed.
"We'll divide what's left of it," Dottie said firmly.
Then the three kittens hugged.

"Oh, dear," Hopper said to himself. He turned away from the kittens—only to find himself nose-to-nose with Sir Byron, the Great Hare!

"Why haven't you delivered to your area?" Sir Byron demanded.

Hopper opened his mouth, but no sound came out. The chocolate that was smeared all over his face said it all.

"Come with me," Sir Byron said.

Hopper followed him to the burrow, and the kittens tagged along behind. Sir Byron gave the kittens what was left of Hopper's goodies and made them honorary Easter bunnies.

"Go now," Sir Byron told the kittens. "Spread joy and love!"

The Great Hare turned to Hopper. "As for you," he said, "you shall watch the kittens hide your treats. Perhaps then you'll understand what it means to be an Easter bunny."

It took a while for the kittens to get the knack of hippety-hopping. But they had no trouble at all spreading joy.

Hopper followed as they crossed the forest, hiding a brightly colored egg here, a chocolate bunny there. He watched as young gophers, squirrels, moles, and mice squeaked with delight as they found their treats.

Hopper looked up and saw the clouds change from pink to fluffy white. He saw the first crocuses open their petals.

Hopper felt a lump in his throat. He'd always just worked his route, then gone home to soak his sore paws. He had never noticed the wonder and magic of Easter before. It made him feel happy inside.

Just then Sir Byron appeared at his side. "What do you think about Easter now, Hopper?"

"It's wonderful!" Hopper said.

From then on, Hopper was glad to be an Easter
bunny. He didn't mind spending every day of the year
making treats for others to enjoy.

And the next year, for the first time in his life,
Hopper was eager for the night before Easter.

Finally the magic night arrived. Hopper's feet felt as light as marshmallow chicks as he danced the Easter bunny dance. He couldn't wait to get his wheelbarrow heaped with treats and hide them all over the woods for happy youngsters to find.

When Sir Byron gave Hopper his wheelbarrow, he said, "Since you have an awfully big route for one little bunny, I've arranged for you to have some helpers."

Hopper laughed as the three little kittens popped out from behind the Great Hare.

And as they pushed their delicious load through the moonlit forest with a *hippety, hoppety, mew, mew, mew,* Hopper realized just how much happiness Easter brings.

The Grumpy Bunny Goes to School,
ISBN-13: 978-0-439-64433-4, ISBN-10: 0-439-64433-X.
Text copyright © 1996 by Justine Korman. Illustrations copyright © 1996 by Lucinda McQueen.

The Grumpy Bunny's Spooky Night,
ISBN-13: 978-0-8167-6611-6, ISBN-10: 0-8167-6611-8.
Text copyright © 2000 by Justine Korman. Illustrations copyright © 2000 by Lucinda McQueen.

Grumpy Bunny's Snowy Day,
ISBN-13: 978-0-8167-4379-7, ISBN-10: 0-8167-4379-7.
Text copyright © 1997 by Justine Korman. Illustrations copyright © 1997 by Lucinda McQueen.

I Love You, Grumpy Bunny,
ISBN-13: 978-0-439-74204-7, ISBN-10: 0-439-74204-8.
Text copyright © 1997 by Justine Korman. Illustrations copyright © 1997 by Lucinda McQueen.

The Grumpy Bunny's Too Many Bunnybabies,
ISBN-13: 978-0-8167-7223-0, ISBN-10: 0-8167-7223-1.
Text copyright © 2002 by Justine Korman. Illustrations copyright © 2002 by Lucinda McQueen.

The Grumpy Easter Bunny,
ISBN-13: 978-0-439-63595-0, ISBN-10: 0-439-63595-0.
Text copyright © 1995 by Justine Korman. Illustrations copyright © 1995 by Lucinda McQueen.

12 11 10 9 8 7 6 5 4 3 2 1   7 8 9 10 11/0

Printed in Singapore   46

ISBN-13: 978-0-545-01099-3
ISBN-10: 0-545-01099-3

First compilation printing, May 2007